For our grandparents and Loris

MYRIAD BOOKS LIMITED
35 Bishopsthorpe Road, London SE26 4PA

First published in 2005 by
MIJADE PUBLICATIONS
16-18, rue de l'Ouvrage
5000 Namur-Belgium

© Isabel Carralo, 2005
© Ronald Molitor, 2005

Translation Lisa Pritchard

ISBN 1 905606 28 1

Printed in China

Ragamuffin

Isabel Carralo

Ronald Molitor

MYRIAD BOOKS LIMITED

It's autumn and Ragamuffin is busy collecting food for the
winter. He has found lots of hazelnuts and acorns, and even
a little red apple.

"Goodness that's heavy,"
he says. "How am I going to ge
all this up into my tree without
dropping it?"

Luckily he finds a sack lying on the ground.

"Perfect!" he exclaims. "I can put it all in this
sack and that will make it easier to carry."

And that's just what he does.

When Ragamuffin looks inside
the sack he can see there is
room for more food. So he
climbs up the nearest tree and
throws in some more nuts.

When he looks down, he's a bit puzzled. The sack doesn't seem to be filling up. "That's odd," he says.

He opens the sack. "Where is that lovely red apple?" he shouts. "And the hazelnuts? And the walnuts?"

He jumps up and down in a rage. Apples don't just get up and walk away by themselves. Nuts don't have legs. Someone must have stolen them.

"How can I catch the thief?"
Ragamuffin thinks to himself.
"Shall I hide behind that tree?
Or maybe in those bushes?"

Then he has a good idea.
"I'll hide in the sack."

"When the thief sees that the sack is full, he'll open it up to see what's inside. And it won't be acorns!"

So Ragamuffin waits in the sack.
And he waits… and waits… then suddenly he
hears a whoosh of feathers.

Someone opens up the sack to take a look.

Ragamuffin shouts, "SO IT WAS YOU! You stole my hazelnuts and acorns and my lovely little red apple!"

"Wow, you scared me!"
shrieks Charlie Chicken.

"What do you mean,
a lovely little red apple?
I just wondered what
was in the sack.
Now I know – it's just a
very grumpy squirrel."

Ragamuffin replies, "You'd be
grumpy too if someone had
stolen all your food."

"Oh dear, is that what's
happened? Well, I'll help
you catch that thief."

Charlie Chicken and
Ragamuffin hide in
the sack together.

They wait… and wait… and wait…
Then suddenly they hear the pitter-patter
of tiny feet. Someone is tiptoeing
towards the sack…

When the sack opens, what do they see? A tiny nose, two tiny eyes and two tiny ears. It's Mini Mouse.

Ragamuffin and Charlie Chicken both shout, "WE'VE GOT YOU!"

Ragamuffin says, "You stole all my nuts and my lovely little red apple, didn't you?"

Mini Mouse exclaims, "I didn't steal anything. That's my sack – so everything in it is mine."

And she grabs the last acorn from the bottom of the bag.

"GIVE IT BACK!" Ragamuffin says loudly.

"Too late," Mini Mouse grins. "I've already taken a bite out of it."

Charlie Chicken tells them to be quiet. "I think there's someone coming!"

All three stand very still and listen.
There it is… the sound of footsteps.
And they are getting closer.

"Quick, let's hide!"
Charlie Chicken whispers.
"Where?" says Ragamuffin.

"In the sack, of course!"
Charlie Chicken replies.

TOO LATE!
Someone's opening up
the sack and he's got big
sharp teeth!

"TIME FOR LUNCH!
How lucky I am,
I've got everything
I need in this sack,"
says Wolfie Wolf.

He sets off with the sack on his back, licking his lips.
"Mmmm, I'll have squirrel for starters, then some
lovely chicken soup, and I'll finish off with
chocolate mouse for
pudding. Yummy!"

.

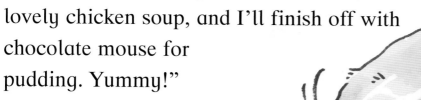

Soon Wolfie Wolf is back
at his den.

But when Wolfie checks his larder, he can't find any chocolate for the chocolate mouse. "Bother! I'll have to go and get some."

As soon as Wolfie is out of the house, Mini Mouse gnaws a hole in the sack and jumps out. "I don't want to be a chocolate mouse," she tells the others.

Mini Mouse unties the string and out jump Ragamuffin and Charlie Chicken. "RUN!" shrieks Charlie Chicken. "RUN! Wolfie will be back very soon." "Yes let's go!" says Ragamuffin. "I don't want him to catch us again, and I certainly don't want to be his first course."

Mini Mouse has other plans. "Wait! Give me a hand with all this food in his larder. We can take it with us. Help me fill up the sack again."

A moment later Wolfie comes through the door. He's very fed up. The shop was closed and he couldn't buy any chocolate. And what's worse, now the sack isn't on the table where he left it…

… and it seems to be running out of the door. Suddenly it dawns on Wolfie… "But… but… STOP! My lunch is getting away!"

It's too late. Wolfie's lunch is already racing down the hill. Ragamuffin, Charlie Chicken and Mini Mouse breathe a sigh of relief.

"What shall we do next?" says Charlie Chicken. "I think we should have some lunch after all our adventures," says Ragamuffin. "Mini Mouse can bring the pudding – after all she's got a lovely little red apple!"

They fetch the apple from Mini Mouse's tiny hole, and then they all lend a hand to store all the food up in Ragamuffin's cosy treehouse. They fold up the sack and leave it at the bottom of the tree.

When everything is up in the tree, the three friends all sit down and eat the best meal they have ever had.

When they had all finished, Ragamuffin said, "Looks like we've got enough food to see us through the winter! Does anyone want a little red apple?"

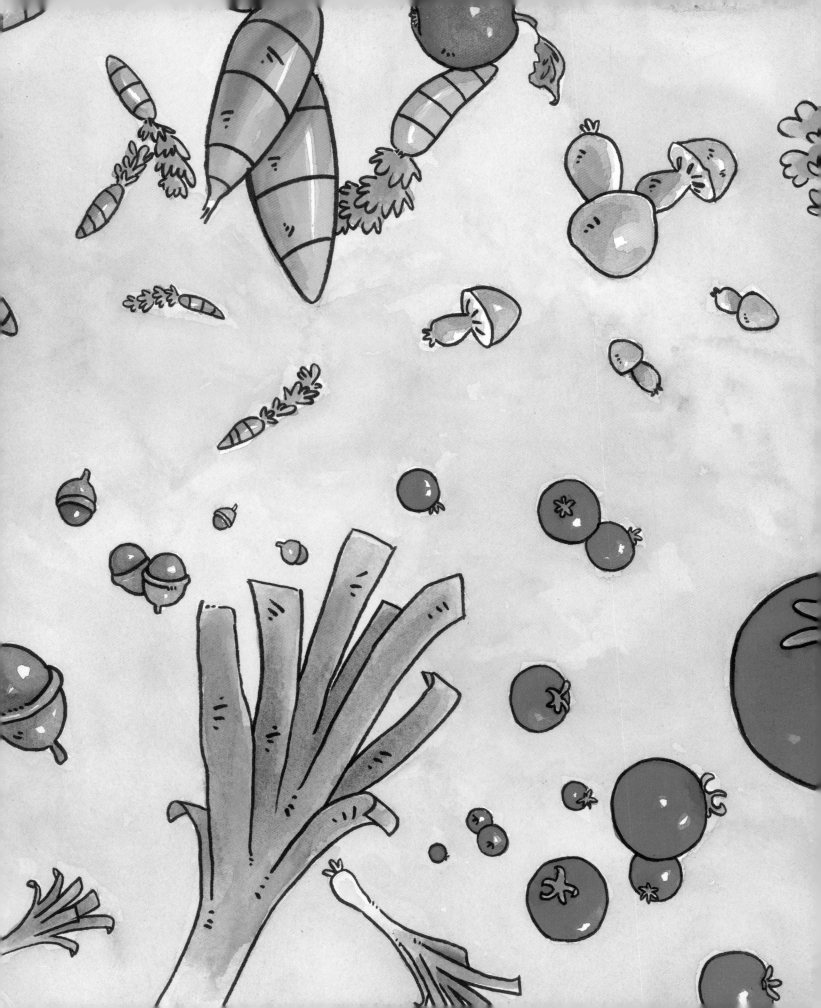

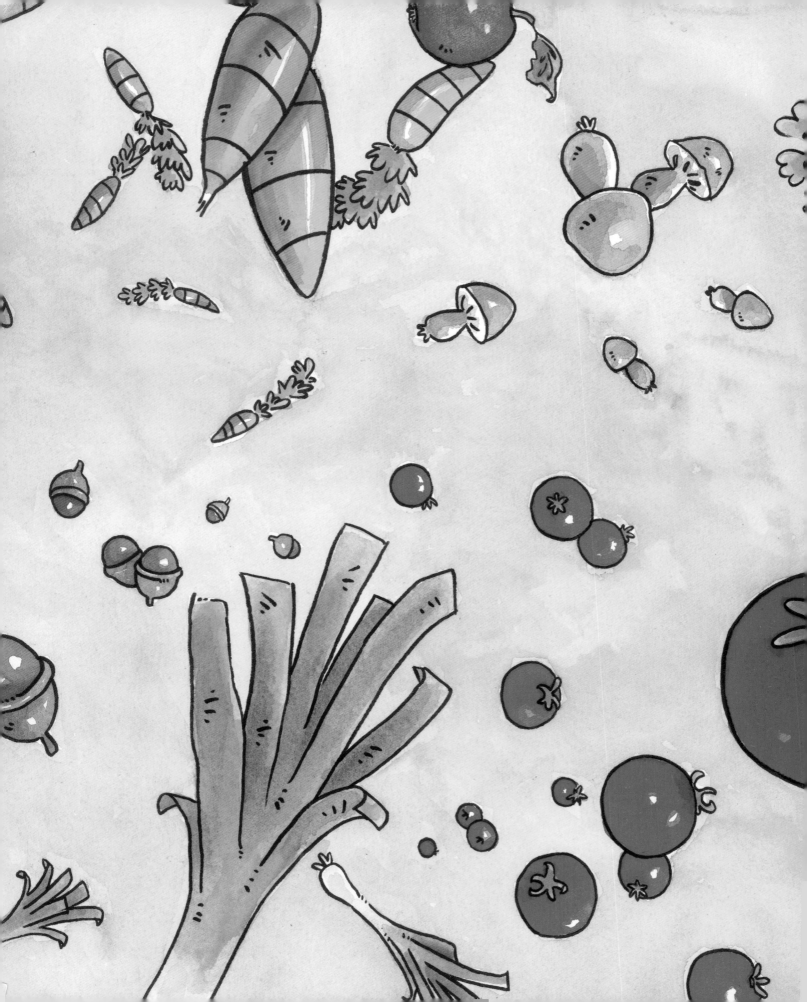